We sleep soundly in our beds because rough men stand ready in the night to visit violence on those who would do us harm.

- George Orwell -

A Million $ Ride

I wouldn't pay a nickel to do again

Kevin P. McGinnis

Table of Contents

Acknowledgments

Preface

Acknowledgments

I want to thank my fellow police officers and support personnel for allowing me to be here to write the stories. You have literally saved my life several times. It is a debt I can never repay.

I am lucky to have had family and friends to accompany me on this ride. Each one of you have shared a part of my story and now I share it all with you.

Thank you Detective Christopher McGinnis and Officer Mark Sunnquist for assisting with the cover photo.

Most of all, this book would not have been possible without the invaluable assistance and guidance from my editor, Pam Rensing. You made this book possible.

Preface

Many years ago, I heard someone describe their law enforcement career as, "A million dollar ride I wouldn't pay a nickel to do again." I know of no better description of the love/hate relationship police officers have with their profession. As I struggled to name my first book, that saying popped into my thoughts and clearly had to become the book title.

For nearly 30 years, I have considered writing a book about my experiences and those of my fellow officers in law enforcement. My delay was not because of a lack of stories to tell but rather how I was going to project the emotional connection that becomes a part of each interaction. I can as easily describe the color yellow to a person that has been blind since birth than be able to make one understand what we do. It is my hope I have chosen the proper words in the proper order to make some connection to the reader.

As you read just a taste of the nearly 40 years of police contacts in my career, I would ask you to take advantage of the written words. It is the lack of visual and auditory inputs provided by reality television programs that makes these books so important in understanding the officer's experience. It allows the mind's eye to make the reader a part of the story and experience first-hand the fear, anger, heartbreak and laughter that are the roller coaster of emotions all of which police officers sometimes experience in just one work shift. I would invite the reader to experience these emotions as we did. Feel free to cry, to be angry or to laugh out loud when appropriate.

The greatest expectation I have with this book is to help the reader understand that it is not the physical aspects of the job that are most difficult but the emotional weight that becomes increasingly more difficult to manage as our careers progress. That is likely why police officers historically have one the highest rates of suicides among any profession.

Because this is my first attempt to present our stories in print, I was selective in the ones I chose so I could limit the length of the book. If A MILLION DOLLAR RIDE is a moderate success, it is my intent to follow with subsequent books. Each story is based upon an actual event but I have taken the liberty to change some of the facts, names of those involved and locations of the event. Not only is this done for legal purposes but to protect the identity of the victims, officers and others involved from any undue publicity.

The guilty deserve no such protections but I have also disguised their identities because they do not deserve any further publicity for their horrendous acts.

I expect there will be those who read the book and "just don't get it." There will also be those who will be critical of how the police operate. Some people just hate the police. If you are one of them, don't read this book. Instead, get a petition and get all your friends to sign it for a national "NO POLICE DAY". Pick out one day of the year and convince the government to lay off all police officers that day (preferably my birthday). Let us all know how that works out for you.

I have dealt with a lot of mean and evil people

many of whom would have killed me if the opportunity was present. Almost to the person, these tough guys all called 9-1-1 at some point in their lives to have the police help them when they were overmatched. Yes, we even help the bad guys!

My experiment with writing begins with this book. Should it be successful, I will attribute that success to my editor, Pam Rensing. She made this easy. I just put the story down on paper and she made sense of it. She asked the questions a reader might ask and offered solutions that made me look like a professional writer. She taught me how to communicate with the written word. It is her journalism background that will be the key to my success and that of the book. Thanks, Pam.

Lone Survivor

I am constantly asked by friends, "What is the most frightening thing you have done?" My first response is, "Standing in front of first graders and answering their questions." After the laugh I receive, I generally tell them there is no "one" thing that is the most frightening but a series of things throughout my career that makes my heart rate increase when I recall them. One of the first "most scared" times came on Memorial Day weekend in the early 1980's.

It was Memorial Day weekend and I had to work. It was one of the things I didn't like about the job – having to work on the holidays. My wife and kids were going to the lake today with friends. I'm sure they were already up and packing their lunch.

Just after shift change at 0630 hours on Sunday morning of Memorial Day weekend, we received a call from a panicked resident living near the eastern boarder of our city. It was not exactly clear what was going on although our dispatcher was able to determine there was someone shot and needed an ambulance, and there was another individual who was armed. We responded quickly to the area, and the three units working coordinated their arrival to ensure the maximum firepower if it was needed.

When we stopped two doors down from the address given to the dispatcher, a female in her mid-fifties wearing a blood soaked nightgown ran down the street toward us. As she approached she was yelling, "He's killing them all." Our heightened sense of danger was only reaffirmed by what we saw and heard from this lady. It took about a minute to calm her down to where she was able to coherently tell us what was happening. What she gave us was not very detailed but we did determine that her thirteen-year-old neighbor girl came to her house with a shotgun wound to her chest and said her father was "killing the whole family." As happens many times in this job information is incomplete at best. We did as we have in the past and acted upon what we knew at that moment.

We moved quickly through backyards to the lady's house to evaluate the girl's wounds and get more information about what happened. As a certified Emergency Medical Technician, I examined the girl's chest wound, covered it with a trauma pad and had the dispatcher send in the paramedics to stabilize and remove the girl to the local trauma center. Before she left she was able to tell me that her father shot her with a shotgun and left her for dead. She said he then went to each of her sibling's rooms and she heard multiple gunshots before she was able to crawl out the basement window to the neighbor's house.

When I looked at the other patrolman and the sergeant by my side, I wondered if they could see the blood had drained from my face and been replaced with a look of fear. I was trying not to show my concern but it was physically impossible to hold back. When I looked at the sergeant, I saw concern but remarkably did not sense fear coming from him. I could not understand at this point in my young career how he could remain so calm in the face of such danger.

 My son and I had a fishing trip scheduled for next weekend. He is only six years old. Will he even understand what happened? I just didn't think today was the day I was going to get killed or I would have given them an extra hug and kiss before I left.

I didn't want to go in that house. I wanted to quit. I wanted to be somewhere other than there. But I couldn't quit. I couldn't run away. I took an oath. I swore to the citizens of the United States and my community that I would protect them from those who visit harm upon them. I'm sure there are many people who don't understand what drives us to act even though the likelihood is that we may die. To me, the oath is my "line in the sand." It is the point when I say "enough-is-enough and we won't let you get away with what you did." It was my oath that sent me in that house.

The sergeant directed the other patrolman to remain outside the house while he and I entered to locate the shooter. I guess being one of the best shooters on the department won me the job of searching for the killer. I was happy my partner did not have to go in the house. We all knew one of the main reasons he remained in a reasonable secure position. It was because if the sergeant and I didn't come out alive, there would be someone to tell the story. What a consolation prize to have been granted.

As we came in the back door, there was a three foot square landing. From it we could either go in the door leading to the kitchen or down the steps to the basement. We chose the basement because it was the first step in a methodical search of the house. As we walked down the bare wooden steps, they creaked a bit. We tried to move somewhat quickly because being on a narrow set of steps was tactically a poor place to be if a gunfight started. There was nowhere to take cover to avoid incoming bullets.

When we got to the basement floor, there was a hallway running directly in front of us with two rooms on the right and one room on the left. The first door we approached was on the right so we stood to the side of the opening and the sergeant turned the door knob and pushed the door quickly open with the tip of his boot. I took a quick peek in the room and saw a young male in his late teens with several shotgun wounds to his chest and face. There was no need to check him for life signs because we knew he was dead. There was no one else in the room.

The next door was the one on the left. It opened to half the basement that had not been renovated. It was just concrete walls and floors. Because it was an open area, I was able to see no one was in there with just a quick glance.

We moved to the last door on the right which was open. I was able to move along the hallway wall and look inside. It was a bedroom. There was blood on the walls and on the floor but no one was there. I believed this was the bedroom of the young girl who escaped the house. I remember her saying she crawled out a basement window.

Now that we had cleared the basement of any suspects we went back upstairs. The sergeant and I paused a moment when we reached the entrance landing before we entered the kitchen area. Though no words were spoken, we knew that when the kitchen door opened, we would begin a journey that could likely end with one or both of us dead. Still, the sergeant reached up from his squatted position, opened the door, and we made entry.

My senses were overwhelmed. My eyes darted quickly across the kitchen and dining room for any sign of the slightest movement. My nose was filled with the familiar smell of burned gunpowder. The silence of the room hurt my ears. There was no sound. No sounds from outside. No sound of people inside. None of the sounds you hear in a house like a clock ticking or the house settling. It was DEAD silence and it hurt my ears.

We moved shoulder to shoulder across the kitchen and dining room to a narrow hallway that ran off to our right. I immediately went from the painful silence in my ears to the distracting pounding of my carotid artery as my heart rate raced. As we moved down the hallway, my non-gun hand moved across the wall to steady my trembling knees. Suddenly, I found my thoughts focusing on how nice the wallpaper was in the hallway. I was so afraid of what we were going to see that my thoughts turned from the ugliness to the quality of the wallpaper in order to give me a moment of relief. Just as quick as the thought came, it went away and I was back in the hunt. Each time I took a step forward with my right foot, I wondered if my left foot would follow. I was that unsure of my ability to fight over my need for flight. Somehow I kept walking forward.

We opened the first door on the left and found twin six-year-old girls with massive head injuries from a shotgun blast. I wanted to throw up but I remembered my academy class instructor who told us that if we vomit at a crime scene, it will be captured in pictures forever and so will our reputation. It was a silly thought considering the circumstances, but still it kept my stomach from rebelling. I breathed heavily through my mouth a few times until the urge subsided. I went back to the hallway with the nice wallpaper.

 The sergeant pushed open the door to the next room and we found two other bodies. They were an eleven-year-old girl and an eight-year-old boy. I wasn't sure at that point how much more I could take. I don't know why my feet didn't just turn around and run away in an involuntary action. But they didn't, and so we approached the last door at the end of the hallway...our deadly light at the end of a hellish tunnel. If the murderous father was still in the house, he had to be in this room. It was the only place left to search.

When we opened that door we found a very steep set of stairs that led to an open bedroom in the attic. This was it. At the top of the stairs we should come face-to-face with the killer. He clearly had nothing to live for and I had everything to lose. I followed the sergeant as we intently and methodically moved upward one step at a time. We strained to hear a sound, to hear anything. In about two steps we should be able to get a look in the room. Please Lord, make him dead. I don't want to die today and I don't want to watch my sergeant die.

We crept forward until we could see the large open room with a bed in the center. A middle aged lady in a nightgown was laying partially on the bed with most of her head missing from a gunshot blast. As we arrived at the top of the stairs my sergeant yelled, "Police" which caused me to nearly urinate myself. I wished he would have warned me before he broke the silence with his command. What he saw was a pair of men's legs visible between the bed and the far wall. We moved quickly to better view the suspect and access the scene. By the shape, size and features of the body, it appeared to be a middle aged man. Likely, the father. He was also - without a shadow of a doubt - dead.

We were unable to see his face because he had

pressed the shotgun into the roof of his mouth and pulled the trigger. Everything above his lower jaw was missing and embedded in the wall. It was over. The sergeant and I would not die today. I inhaled deeply and exhaled to release a tension and stress I had not known before, and would only experience a few more times in my career.

While one part of the story was over, another part was ready to begin. Now that we had secured the house, the enormity of what happened here began to register in my conscious thoughts. Seven peoples' lives ended violently here in the house where I now stood. I needed to get outside if for no other reason than to re-establish my connection to the living. There was nothing but evil flowing through this house.

Soon other officers and detectives arrived on scene for the processing and removal of the bodies. I never went back in the house. I had seen a lifetime of violence and death, and I did not need to go back inside to recall what I saw. It played with all too much clarity in my mind but it was only the first of the numerous horror shows that would intersect with my career.

After an exhaustive investigation it was determined that the father's farm that was located several miles outside the city was failing and he decided to take his life. Investigative interviews with the father's siblings and close friends revealed comments he had made concerning his failing farm and thoughts of suicide. Not one of them "took him seriously". Without talking to any other family member, the father had decided they would be better off if they died with him that day. All but one of them did.

Five years and two days later Jamie, the lone survivor, walked across the stage at her high school and received her diploma. Tears flowed across her cheeks as I'm sure thoughts of her siblings filled her mind. She was awarded a scholarship to the University of Illinois and departed later that summer to continue her education. I lost track of her after that summer but I'm confident guardian angels still walk with her.

I truly believe there are people and places that are havens for evil. This house was one of those places. During the next fifteen years another murder/suicide would occur in the house before it burned to the ground taking three more lives. No house was ever rebuilt on the property...thank God.

Enjoy Your Visit

In the early 1980s, many police departments had an issue with gasoline thefts because of the huge jump in price created by the OPEC embargo. We received many calls from residents regarding thieves siphoning gasoline from cars late at night, but most of the thefts were designated as "failure to pay." This was the term used when someone would pump gasoline into their car at a gas station and drive off without paying.

In the early morning hours of a cool fall night, I had such a call.

A local service station attendant reported that a black male in a blue Chevelle failed to pay for ten dollars of gasoline, and was last seen traveling north towards the adjoining community of Rivertown.

Normally this would not be a hard case to solve. I would just call on the radio to the officer on duty in the next community, give him a vehicle and suspect description, and within a few minutes he would spot the car and make a traffic stop.

That's pretty simple, straight forward police work. However...

The entire call may have happened just that way if it was not for who was patrolling the streets and protecting the citizens of Rivertown.

A brief background on the Village of Rivertown might help one to understand the area. Rivertown consisted of about 80 residences with a total population of just under 200 people. However, the work population at any given time was about 8000 people due primarily to the five large chemical and industrial plants in Rivertown.

Their police department at that point was part time and was manned by individuals that would likely not qualify to work at any professional agency anywhere!

On that particular night, Officer Brownly was on duty because it was his day off from his auto mechanic job.

Brownly had spent many of his years working on race cars and subsequently lost a good portion of his hearing.

I had to call Brownly on the radio several times before he finally answered. I informed him of the failure to pay, the blue Chevelle, and the black male driver.

His response? "Who is being blackmailed?"

Trying not to sound unprofessional by laughing on the radio, I spoke louder and slower, and repeated the information. He responded with a "10-4."

I guess he got the information. Anyway, I did my part by broadcasting the information.

Within two minutes I heard Brownly calling on the radio with the high-pitched sound of his siren wailing in the background. He advised our dispatcher he was in pursuit of the suspect vehicle from the failure to pay report. He indicated he was northbound leaving his town and approaching the bridge that adjoins a neighboring state.

I attempted to intervene on the radio and tell Brownly to discontinue the pursuit because the event did not warrant getting someone seriously hurt. By the time I had an opportunity to talk on the radio, Brownly said he had the vehicle stopped on the bridge just across the state line.

I raced to Brownly's location. As I neared the traffic stop, I started noticing car parts in the roadway that eventually led to the vehicle he had stopped.

I was more shocked to see the car Brownly had stopped was a silver Toyota sedan. At least I thought it was a Toyota. It was a bit unrecognizable because the entire car was damaged from Brownly sideswiping it with his police car and then running it into the concrete bridge abutment. There was smoke and steam coming from under the hood, and every fluid in the car was now pouring onto the bridge surface.

I thought to myself, "What a mess! How did he misunderstand what I told him?"

I exited my car and hurried toward Brownly who was quick to introduce the vehicle's occupants.

There standing before me was a small-statured, middle aged man and woman of Oriental decent. Both were obviously agitated, and I did not understand any of the language they were speaking that was increasing at a faster and louder level.

By this time anyone could get the gist of what they were trying to say from their inflamed tone and demeanor. When they started frantically pointing at Brownly, I knew somehow they were saying, "Get us away from this crazy bastard."

I motioned to the tourists in the international "shut the hell up" finger to my closed lips and they paused their infernal noise although their fury was still simmering. I walked to Brownly and told him that this was NOT the car I asked him to stop and these people were NOT the suspects I wanted.

Brownly slowly walked to his patrol car and removed a notebook from the front seat. He looked at it a moment then flipped the page and said, "Oh, that's what happened. I wrote it down in my notebook and when I threw it on the seat the page flipped over to the information I wrote down at a traffic crash last week. You're right. It is the wrong car."

While I was already rehearsing my explanation of the event to the Chief in my head, Brownly calmly walked over to the couple and said, "You should get your car off the bridge because somebody might hit it." With no regrets whatsoever, he sauntered to his police car, and drove away.

I paused for a moment, looked at the surprised twosome and said, "Enjoy your visit," took a couple of bows in their direction - hoping that was the proper thing to do - then promptly got in my car and left.

As I was crossing back across the bridge to my city, I saw a police car from the next state pulling up to the accident scene. As it did, the oriental family was rushing towards it with their mouths opening and closing faster than PacMan. I chuckled and drove on. I never spoke to the Chief about the incident because I was sure there were some things he would rather not know.

...and tell me it's raining

When I was in the U.S. Army, I learned to drink and appreciate coffee. Since becoming a police officer, I've spent many a cold winter's night driving around in my squad car drinking the hot stuff to keep me company. The only drawback was making frequent stops to take a leak. Generally this could be done on a quiet back road but every now and then I needed to go but couldn't stop until after I finished an assignment. For the most part, stopping to urinate does not make for an entertaining story to tell at parties, except for one notable exception.

It was a freezing night shift in the middle of January. I had already consumed enough coffee to make an insomniac jealous. The shift had been slow up to the point when I was assigned as an assist car on an "attempt to locate" call. Generally we receive these calls because a family member has failed to hear from their relative for an extended amount of time. It could be anytime from 12 hours to 12 months. If they lived far away, I could have felt a little more understanding of their situation. However, most of the time the family found it much easier to call the local police and have us tell "Uncle Fred" to call rather than get off their lazy asses, act like they really care, and go knock on his door. The call we received was to a small residential area that consisted of several burned out buildings and some occupied homes that were not fit for habitation.

I arrived about the time as the assigned unit. The house had no utilities, a broken front door, and plastic trash bags for windows. On top of that, when I shined my light into the dark house, I could see about a foot of garbage on the kitchen floor, and rats darting around and through the debris. Damn, I hate rats. That being said, we went inside the house.

We began to look around but it wasn't long before the combination of frigid conditions and a bladder full of coffee made me start looking for a place to take leak. I told my partner I was going to go out back and relieve myself. Even as I was saying this, I was wondering why I should step outside. Surely some fresh urine in the kitchen would not diminish the resale value of this fine vacation home nor bother the rats.

I stepped outside, walked to the backyard, and

started to urinate against the back side of the house but something was amiss. Being a seasoned veteran of outdoor urination, I noticed an unusual amount of splatter hitting my boots. Was I the proverbial cow pissing on a flat rock? What was causing this disturbing deflection? Having multitasking skills in both urination and illumination, I reached for my flashlight, pressed the on switch and screeched like a school girl on a playground who just had her dress blown up by a gust of wind.

My shriek was loud enough to make my partner come running. I'm sure the sight he saw caused many sleepless nights and maybe even more psychotherapist appointments. There I stood like the Statue of Liberty illuminated in the dark night with the exception that I had a flashlight in one hand and my penis in the other. He glanced down and there by my shoes was the body of Uncle Fred. He was frozen to the ground with an ear full of urine that was already beginning to freeze. I looked at my partner and he said, "I have no idea what to say. I don't think anyone would believe me if I told them about this." We both had a chuckle and agreed we would keep this event to ourselves (and the three people who buy this book).

A short time later the coroner arrived and pronounced Uncle Fred as deceased, a victim of natural causes. I heard him wonder out loud about the strange frozen yellow substance found in Uncle Fred's ear. I just gave him the "I don't know" shoulder shrug and left the area.

Double Jeopardy

In basic legal terms, "Double Jeopardy" means a person cannot be tried again for an offense after having been acquitted or found not guilty. It is a protected right under the Fifth Amendment of the United States Constitution. One week in early May of 1982, I came to discover a case of Double Jeopardy as it related to a victim. Through a complete lack of common sense or decency, the State of Illinois became implicit in the death of an elderly man in my city.

I was working as a patrol officer on dayshift and was dispatched to 109 Lemay. The neighbors were concerned for the well-being of the eighty-one year old male resident, John Begner, because the grass had not been mowed and mail was piling up in the mailbox. I drove towards the location but was not in a hurry because almost every call such as this one has a logical explanation.

When I arrived, I was met by a neighbor

who apologized for calling. She said she just realized John's car was gone. She said he most likely went to his daughter's house located about an hour away and neglected to tell any of the neighbors. I told her since I was here anyway I would take a look around the house. I also asked her if she could get the daughter's telephone number so I could confirm that John Begner was alright. She nodded and said she would be right back.

I started at the front door and found it was locked. The living room curtains were drawn so I was unable to see into the house. I continued to walk through the attached carport and to the back door. It was also locked and I could not see through those curtains either. As I got to the rear bedroom window I found what we in law enforcement call a "clue." There were hundreds of flies on the inside of the bedroom window.

The one thing I learned during any homicide investigation was not to draw conclusions on what you hear and see until you understand what you have. I called on the radio for the detectives to come to the scene. At this point, I knew I had something inside that was rotting. Though it may be an elderly man, it was also quite likely left-over food on the stove or counter which caused the multitude of flies.

While I waited for the arrival of the detectives, I again made contact with the neighbor. She gave me the telephone number of John's daughter and I called her. When she answered I identified myself and asked her if John was with her. She said she had not heard from him in a few days but that he should be home. I told her of the high grass and mail surplus. I also told her the doors to the house were locked and his car was not under the carport. I did not mention the hundreds of flies.

The daughter was more puzzled about the situation than concerned but said she could arrive at the house within an hour. I asked her that if we determined a need, could we make a forced entry into the house. She said absolutely.

About that time, the detectives arrived and I brought them up to date on what I knew. We looked at the rear window, decided we would force it open, and go then go inside to investigate the source of the flies.

The window ledge was about five feet from the ground. I turned to look at the two detectives standing next to me. One was in his late fifties and the other was about my age but nearly three hundred pounds. I was a buck sixty five at best. I knew that determining who went through the window would not be accomplished by drawing straws.

I took off my gun belt and shoved my gun in my waistband. One detective pried the window open and the other cupped his hands so I could put my foot in it to be lifted up. As I balanced my body on the window sill and poked my head inside the bedroom, I was met by the distinct pungent odor of rotting flesh. My heart started rapidly beating. I knew this situation was not going to have a happy ending.

As I was pushed into the room, I fell onto a queen size bed and rolled to the floor. I grabbed my gun from my waistband and pointed it towards the bedroom door. I am not embarrassed to say I was scared. I strained to hear something...anything. But the only sound I could detect was the painful pounding of my heart in my chest.

I decided to quickly search the building and minimize the amount of time I was alone in the house. I cleared all three bedrooms and a bathroom, and stepped quietly down the hall towards the living room.

As I stepped into the living room, I noticed a slight movement out of the corner of my right eye near the front entrance door. I instantly turned and pointed my firearm looking across the sights mounted on top. What I saw was a rotting corpse so filled with maggots that it actually appeared to be moving. Because of the heat that had built up in the house, the body had grown to three times its normal size with the additional increase being bodily fluids and gases.

My gag reflex kicked in. I knew I had to get out of the house and into some fresh air...immediately! The shortest way, and least likely to disturb a possible crime scene, was to go out the front door. The problem? There a rotting body about three feet high between me and freedom.

There was not a lot of time for decision making in this matter because I was less than thirty seconds away from vomiting on the crime scene. No greater embarrassment can follow an officer throughout his/her career than for other officers to know you lost-your-lunch at a crime scene especially when it would be permanently preserved in photographs displayed in court files.

This was it. My decision was made. I took two steps back and then ran towards the body, hurdling it as if I were participating in an Olympic sport. Without disturbing the crime scene, I unlocked the door, threw it open, and went coughing and spitting into the front yard.

I bent over, my hands on my knees. I gasped for fresh air while pleading with the contents of my stomach to stay down. A lady then walked up to me and said she was John's daughter. She asked me if I found John dead inside the house. I thought it seemed pretty obvious since I was gagging and sweating profusely. But I was able to nod my head in the affirmative. She hesitantly stepped back. Maybe she was stunned or wasn't sure how to react. I couldn't help her at that point. Fortunately she was comforted by the neighbor and led away.

I took a few minutes and gathered myself. I spoke with the detectives and the immediate cause of death appeared to be natural causes. But as I said before, it is not good to draw conclusions about what happened until all the evidence is examined. I reminded them that if this was a "natural cause death" scene then where was John Begner's car? A missing car did not fit the scenario.

We went back in the house to look for more

clues as to what transpired a few days earlier. That walk through helped us tremendously because we discovered the door of the gas oven was open and there was blood on the door. A quick test showed it was human blood. Also John's wallet, containing an unknown amount of cash, and several credit cards were missing along with his checkbook. The daughter told us where he kept his car keys and they were also missing. This was looking more like a homicide than a natural death.

We called the coroner to the scene to pronounce John legally dead as required by Illinois law. I went back in the house with the coroner to observe his examination. I saw him remove a surgical knife from his tool kit. I knew what was coming next but I was not at liberty to leave the crime scene. The coroner slashed the swollen body across the abdomen which caused a release of bodily gases and fluids that filled the room. If that weren't enough for those with a weak stomach, he took his latex gloved hand and scooped several handfuls of maggots from the body so he could do a closer examination. Within a few minutes the coroner located a large gash across John's forehead that appeared to result in a skull fracture. He also determined by the postmortem lividity (pooling of blood in relation to gravity), it was obvious something had been tied around his wrists to restrain him.

At this point in the initial investigation, there was enough preliminary evidence to work this case as a homicide. The body was removed for an autopsy by the local forensic pathologist. This would reveal more crucial information. We decided to request the Major Case Squad be activated to handle the investigation.

The Major Case Squad is a collection of highly trained investigators who work for police departments in a nine county area in southern Illinois and Missouri. They can be activated on short notice, and are usually at the crime scene in less than two hours. Their departments pay them and the requesting agency is only responsible for providing fuel for their vehicles, food for the officers, and giving them a work area.

Their solve rate on homicides during the last thirty years is over 95 percent. They have proven invaluable in assisting smaller police agencies with resources and knowledge that would be otherwise absent. Having the Major Case Squad take over a case brings in much needed manpower to follow leads in a timely manner before they grow cold.

About an hour after the body was removed from the crime scene, Doctor Patel began the autopsy at a local hospital. While awaiting the preliminary results, investigators began a neighborhood canvas. Neighborhood canvases are generally a good starting point in these types of investigations. More often than not someone observes something that at the time appeared normal but now takes on a suspicious tone. In the case of the murder of John Begner, the neighborhood canvas gave us the most valuable lead.

When talking to a woman who lived across the street from Begner, she recounted seeing a sixteen-year-old boy that lived two doors down and a middle aged man who just moved in with his sister next door to Begner. They were seen by her two days earlier coming out of Begner's house and leaving in his car. She told us she thought this was a bit unusual but rationalized that John was just allowing the man to borrow his car. The detectives then began to concentrate on the two houses to locate and identify the boy and man.

It was learned from the father of the sixteen-year-old that the teen had been hanging around Zeth Baxter who was the older brother of Joanne Zeizer. The father said Joanne had told him she was concerned for his son's safety because Baxter had spent some time in prison. She did not tell him why he had been imprisoned. He said everywhere Baxter went his son went so it was likely they are together now.

The father also said he hadn't seen his son

in two days and was going to report him missing if he did not come home tonight. We knew this was a lie and he was only trying to justify why he allowed his child to be gone for two days.

At the same time, detectives were interviewing Joanne Zeizer who told officials she had always been fearful of her brother and was especially so when he moved in to live with her a few months ago. She said Baxter was released from prison in Pontiac, Illinois about three months ago. He was convicted of killing an elderly neighbor in northern Illinois in 1970. He was sentenced to death but the United States Supreme Court ruled the death penalty unconstitutional in 1972 and his sentence was commuted to life in prison.

Now common sense would dictate that if a person's death penalty was commuted and changed to "life" that would be interpreted as the person remaining in prison until their life ends. But that was not the case with Zeth Baxter. His life sentence was "life with parole." Wouldn't you think if a jury decided Zeth's crimes were serious enough to terminate his life that the default position would be "life without parole?"

No one in the decision making process involving Baxter's future seemed to comprehend the unfairness toward society this decision represented. That decision was no longer an abstract idea but had manifested itself in the form of John Begner's maggot covered body. It was my opinion that the State of Illinois committed double jeopardy against its citizens by not adequately punishing Baxter for killing one of its citizens but releasing him to do it again. That's insane!

As the investigation continued, it was determined the juvenile and Baxter had restrained Begner and beat him about his head. They then forced his head into a gas oven until he succumbed to the attack. They took two credit cards, several hundred dollars in cash, and Begner's car. The next step in the investigation was clear to the homicide investigators. If Baxter used the credit cards, it would amount to leaving a trail of crumbs to his location. Contact was made with both credit card companies.

Because this was the early 1980s, the ability to follow purchases in "real time" was not yet available. At best, we could track the purchase anywhere between several hours to several days after the transaction. Because Baxter and the juvenile had a two day head start, we were able to obtain enough information to get a general idea where they had been but not enough to know precisely where they were going.

Purchases in Clarksville and Chattanooga, Tennessee on the first day were followed by a night at a hotel in Macon, Georgia and fuel in Ocala, Florida on the second day. This was day three of their flight but neither credit card company had a record of any purchases that day.

The car had been entered as "stolen in homicide" in NCIC (National Crime Information Center) and direct calls had been made to the Florida and Georgia

Bureaus of Investigation to alert their troopers. There was nothing to do but wait for the next lead. Luckily it came within a few hours.

It appeared Baxter was becoming more comfortable with using Begner's credit cards because the purchases became more frequent and began to occur every couple of hours. To complicate the search however, Baxter abandoned driving the interstate highways and was now driving secondary roads. If we were to capture Baxter and the juvenile, the investigators needed to determine where they were going.

The best way to determine that was to learn more about Baxter, and his family and friends. Once we knew him, we could get inside his head and think like him.

We compiled an extensive background on Baxter. We weren't sure why Baxter headed south towards Florida, but the collective consensus was he would eventually go to his older sister's house in northern Illinois. Two teams of investigators packed some clothes and left immediately for the sister's house in Quincy, Illinois. We decided not to inform the sister about our surveillance as we were unsure of her relationship with Baxter.

Within four hours the teams had arrived in Quincy and checked into a local motel. They made contact with the Illinois State Police Criminal Investigations Division, and advised them of the stake out and the need for their assistance in taking Baxter into custody should he appear at the address. The teams alternated eight hour shifts over the next three days.

During this time they were updated from the Major Case Command Center as Baxter's credit card purchases led him back north through Georgia and Tennessee. The most recent purchase was in Paducah, Kentucky. They were clearly heading back.

Our theory that Baxter was heading towards his sister's house in Quincy seemed on point. But just in case we were wrong, the Squad Commander placed several teams on a twenty four hours surveillance of the juvenile's house, Joanne Zeizer's house, and the murder scene in case Baxter decided to sneak back in town.

On the third day of the investigation, day five after the murder, the surveillance team in Quincy observed two people in Begner's car pull into the driveway of his sister's home. As the two got out of the car, they looked around to see if anyone was watching. They didn't see the detectives a block down the road but the detectives saw them - the two suspects wanted for heinous murder John Begner. They made a call to the Commander of the Major Case Squad to inform him they had spotted the suspects.

The commander told them to get the other team back on site. He also notified the Illinois State Police Criminal Investigations to send several more investigators to the scene to create a secure perimeter. Since it was early afternoon, the commander also sent three more teams from the command center to Quincy.

It was determined we would seek an arrest

warrant for Baxter and the juvenile, and visually secure the house until sometime after midnight. They felt a late night entry would catch the suspects sleeping and decrease any chance of a violent encounter. It also reduced the chances of innocent bystanders being present in the neighborhood.

Contained restlessness grew as we knew it was just a matter of hours until the suspects were in custody. What did not escape us was the danger that was always present when arresting a violent offender. We all knew that tragedy could happen in the blink of an eye.

Each officer donned their tactical body armor and insured all their equipment was functional. Now it was time to sit and wait. The commander contacted us and indicated he had secured arrest warrants for Baxter and the juvenile. The Illinois State Police Tactical Response Team arrived at a school about a mile away and began to formulate entry and arrest plans. Fire rescue and EMS were also dispatched to the school as we prepared for any contingency.

At 2300 hours, we met in the school cafeteria for a final briefing. Everyone involved in the operation was present. The tactical team told us where they would enter the house and prepared us for the noise of the flash bangs (explosive concussion devices) that would precede their entry by about three seconds.

If everything went as planned, the tactical team would be the only people to enter the house until the suspects were in custody and the "clear" sign was given. The Major Case detectives would secure a perimeter around the property to insure no one escaped the house.

We had a plan. Now we needed to get all these police officers, fire equipment, and ambulances to the area without waking up the entire neighborhood. I've been part of these types of operations before and we have learned to operate in a stealth mode at least until the flash bangs go off and the entry team start yelling, "Police Officers, arrest warrant." From that point, the entire neighborhood is awake and the perimeter set up by the Major Case Squad becomes more about keeping inquisitive spectators away.

By 0005 hours, all units were in place around the house. A last radio check of all units was broadcasted through my earpiece. It was time. I was nervous, but it was a healthy nervous. The entry team began to strike the front door with a battering ram as the team leader yelled, "Police Officers, we have an arrest warrant."

By the third blow of the battering ram, the front door flew open and was quickly followed by a brilliant light coming out of the windows and doors of the house, and the sound and feeling of a strong concussion that could be felt a block away.

Within a few seconds another flash bang went off, and then fifteen to twenty seconds of eerie silence followed. The next thing we heard was several voices yelling, "clear" and the team walking Baxter and the juvenile out the front door in handcuffs.

It was over.

The next day detectives attempted to interview Baxter who immediately "lawyered up" and decided not to talk to us. However, the juvenile did talk and related the entire sequence of events from the murder to their arrest. A deal was made with the juvenile's attorney that he would testify against Baxter in exchange for being charged with Concealing a Homicidal Death, a charge that eventually disappeared from his record when he turned eighteen years old.

The trial began about thirteen months later and lasted for two weeks. Baxter was found guilty and sentenced to Life WITHOUT parole. Had the State of Illinois originally commuted Baxter's sentence to life without parole in 1972, Mr. John Begner would have still been alive. He would have spent his days talking to his neighbors, visiting with his daughter, and basically enjoying life. Instead he became the innocent victim of a state sponsored Double Jeopardy.

Blind Justice?

Unlike many of the television crime dramas, I have never been involved in a trial in which the prosecuting attorney hammers questions at the defendant until they finally "come clean" and admit to everything they did in the presence of a packed court room. It makes for good television viewing but is far from reality. In the many trials I have been a witness, there is one particular trial I found myself looking around the courtroom waiting for the hidden camera to be revealed and told I am being "pranked". It was, in fact, a real trial with real people and a real victim and suspect but this justice was not blind.

The trial surrounded an event that began in August of the previous year when I conducted a felony traffic stop on a main highway in my city. The driver was stopped because an area broadcast was made by a neighboring county to be on the lookout (BOLO) for a light blue pickup truck with a couch in the truck bed and being driven by a white male named Jimmie Workman. Workman was reportedly wanted for residential burglary. I spotted the truck, ran a check on the license plates and found they were registered to Workman. The felony stop went without incident and Workman was taken into custody. He was later transported to the county south of my city in which the offense happened and held on the felony charge. He remained in custody until the trial date because he was unable to post the $10,000 cash bond.

It was now mid-April, some eight months after the alleged offense and the trial was to begin on Wednesday of that week. I met on Monday with the county prosecutor, Willie Freeman, to go over my upcoming testimony in the case. As if he were practicing for his presentation to the jury, he laid out his case to me. Workman was accused of entering a vacant residence in which the owner had moved nearly all their property out to their new residence. He removed and later confessed to taking a clear glass mason jar containing approximately 500 pennies without the owner's permission. I waited to hear what other things he took but the attorney stopped at that point because that was the extent of Workman's crime. Freeman said he made an offer to Workman and his attorney that would have allowed him to plead guilty in exchange for a 20 year sentence. That is one year for every quarter dollar he took. I was shocked at the offer but I should have seen it coming. Workman was from my area in Harrison County and he committed the offense in Lincoln County. It was no secret the residents of the mostly rural Lincoln County did not like "outsiders" coming from the "big city" and victimizing them. Their criminal justice system reflected their fears and desire to inflict a harsh punishment on those who would venture in from the outside. I silently wondered if the jar Workman took might have been large enough to contain twenty dollars in change would he now be facing a life sentence? After the short meeting I left Freeman's office to return for the trial at 9:00 a.m. on Wednesday.

I arrived at the Lincoln County Courthouse in full police uniform at 8:30 on Wednesday. The courthouse had been converted from an old school house. The only courtroom seated about 50 people in individual wooden chairs similar to the ones my teachers sat in during the 1960's. The jury box had more updated padded chairs and the judges bench looked like a circa 1950's headmasters desk. The witness chair sat at the end of his desk to his right with the jury on his left.

At 9:15, I was called from the hallway to the witness stand. I stood before the court clerk and was sworn to tell the truth. I sat in the witness chair and was asked to introduce myself. As I did, I looked toward the jury as it is appropriate to address them directly. As I began to introduce myself I noticed one of the jurors waiving to me in a motion I would describe as one operating a hand puppet. I looked directly in her face and recognized her as Jean my childhood neighbor and baby sitter. It had been at least 20 years since I had seen her but we recognized each other. After completing my introduction I motioned for Mr. Freemen to come to the witness stand. As he leaned over to me I explained my relationship with who I later found to be the jury foreman. He turned and explained the situation to Judge Meyer who asked my friend, Jean, in open court, if she recognized and knew me. She chuckled and said she did and that I was a "very nice and polite young man and always told the truth". Judge Meyer turned to Mr. Freeman and said, "I don't see a problem. Continue with the trial".

Mr. Freeman asked me his first question concerning my probable cause for the traffic stop I conducted on Mr. Workman. As I began to explain how I monitored a radio broadcast indicating the information on Workman's want, the defense attorney objected on grounds the broadcast was "hearsay". I knew from case law he was correct but Mr. Freemen attempted to argue his case against the objection. Judge Meyers told counsel to leave the room and discuss how the testimony would proceed while a short recess would take place. Counsel left the room and everyone else remained seated.

In an attempt to avoid eye contact with Jean, I looked around the courtroom. At some point I realized Judge Meyers was looking directly at me. I turned to him and he gave me a "thumbs up" sign. I know I thought but surely did not say out loud, "You've gotta be shittin' me" or I would have been held in contempt of court. I then did a mental review of the situation. Mr. Freeman offered Workman a year in prison for every 25 cents he took. The jury foreman would have believed me if I declared Workman an alien visitor from a galaxy far, far away and the judge just showed up so he could declare the defendant "guilty". I think that's a pretty fair assessment of the situation. The trial continued for about another hour and in the end Workman was found guilty and sentenced to 10 years in prison which reduced his sentence from 25 cents per year to 50 cents per year. Before I left the courtroom, the defense attorney filed a verbal appeal against the sentence.

As I walked to my car in the parking lot I was still somewhat expecting a camera crew to appear in my path and declare this a prank but it did not happen. I drove back to my department and before I could tell them what happened in my trial, they were excited about a plea negotiation in a murder we had handled several years prior. In that case, the suspect made the victim kneel down and beg for his life before he shot him three times in the back of the head. The plea was for **10 years**. I wondered if the murder victim would have had 500 pennies in his pocket if the sentence would have doubled. There was nothing "blind" about justice on this day. Just a severe case of myopia.

A Lot of Manure

At times the police are the only means of contact by citizens to their local government. Because we work throughout the night, weekends, holidays and generally all the time, people call us with every type of problem one could imagine. In particular, I hated when we received the Animal Control calls after normal business hours. I will tell you that my regional Animal Control department would not come out after hours if Godzilla was eating the electrical power grid. Police officers do their best to resolve the animal situation or at least put a band-aid on it until normal business hours resumed.

On a particularly warm summer evening, I received a call from dispatch to respond to an "animal complaint." Who knew what that meant? But I did recognize the neighborhood as the one we called "Deliverance." It reminded us of the backwoods, uneducated hillbillies from the movie. At times I swear I could hear banjo music playing in the background.

Last time I was there, I was met by a sixteen-year-old pregnant girl with a cigarette hanging from her mouth, and motor oil on her hands, face and clothes. She was mad because she pulled out the motor in the neighbor's car and rebuilt it. She was yelling, "And now the guy's trying to fuck me over and not pay me." She was typical of those who lived in the area.

When I arrived, I was met by a middle aged, unshaven, unbathed, bib overall wearing, three-toothed, limited vocabulary "taxpayer." He rushed toward my police car before I could get out. He was so excited he had to pause for a moment, bend over at the waist with his hands on his knees, and inhale deeply before he began his laborious rant again. I wasn't sure exactly what had happened, but I gathered he wanted me to come into his house. We walked towards his house as he continued to speak in tongues only perceptible by swamp people.

As I neared the open front door of his house, I smelled the familiar aroma of digested hay. In particular...horse manure. I stepped through the door, lost my footing but quickly grabbed onto the door frame only to find it also was covered with the same substance...fragrant horse manure.

Even before I could visually scan the area, my

expert powers of deduction told me there must be a horse nearby. I guess that is what made me less surprised when I saw a dead horse lying on its side in the living room. Not a piece of furniture remained intact. Everything was crushed by the weight of the mount. Adding to the already uncommon event were the results of the pressure release from the horse's bowels. It covered everything including a thirty-year-old family portrait which now had the mullet wearing matriarch sporting a manure mustache, much like an Etch-a-Sketch.

Next came the million dollar question. What was the horse doing in the house?

The owner explained he was out riding the horse and it appeared to become overheated. The owner said he brought the horse into the air conditioned house to cool down but it suddenly fell over dead.

He asked what we were going to do next. I told him "WE" did not have a problem, "HE" did.

Nonetheless I decided to offer some assistance. This being my first dead horse in a house, I pondered a solution. I decided we would call a "zone tow" (an assigned tow truck) to remove the horse from the house.

About twenty minutes later, the tow truck arrived. As though he had removed dozens of dead horses from living rooms before, the driver went about the task of removing the horse without as much as a "What the hell" crossing his lips. He put a cable around the horse and winched it from the house to the front yard. The owner then asked what we were going to do next. I told him I was going to get in my car and leave, and he could call Animal Control in the morning to ask what they would do.

It was when I got back in my car I first realized that I not only had horse manure in the treads of my boots but also on my uniform shirt and pants. I smelled like a horse trainer. It was a long and aromatic ride back to the station to shower and change to a clean uniform. Even more interesting was the explanation to my wife when I came home with a uniform full of manure under my arm. She gave her standard reply......"Whatever!"

But Sarge, it rhymed

I've found that many of the best cops are those who have "street sense," not just a formal education. The only problem with the lack of language and writing skills is that no matter how great a job we do, it all comes down to how well we write the report.

A good report must contain the who, what, where, when, why, and how of an event. And even when all those questions are answered, it is as much about the writing technique as it is the information presented.

I would like to sight a report submitted by a good officer with limited writing skills. He was assigned to check on two suspicious persons in a car parked behind a closed business late at night. His report read;

"Janet Becker from Steckler was sucking her husband's pecker."

It was only one sentence long and it provided the

information needed for a report but it didn't quite meet the reporting requirements set by our department.

When the report was sent back to the officer for rewrite, his only defense was "But Sarge, it rhymed."

I Didn't Do This

I am constantly asked what the most horrifying thing I have experienced in the five decades I have served as a police officer. There is no "terror" scale that helps to organize the horrible sights that we, as police officers, witness. It is difficult to rank one homicide or death uglier than another. All death scenes are tragic in their own way and one is not more important than another.

If I were required under oath to pick out one particular deadly event that was the most shocking to me, it would be the Duncan murders in May of 1978. It surely was not the most heinous or gruesome murder scene I have examined but it was the first violent death I experienced in my career and it had the most impact upon me.

It was a sunny and humid weekday morning in late May '78. Most people in this Midwestern blue collar community were in the process of heading off for another day's work. Generally the police would handle a few property damage calls and a fender-bender or two, maybe conduct some traffic enforcement on a normal weekday. I did not know that peaceful weekday morning that this would become anything but "normal." Two people had been killed, their bodies yet to be discovered.

The call came in about 6:45 a.m. from a woman who stated she babysits for Linda Duncan who lives in the 300 block of Sycamore Street. She was concerned because Linda was always on time dropping off her five-year-old son, Bryce. She told the dispatcher Linda was late. When she called her home there was no answer. The caller asked if an officer could go by the residence and check on Linda and Bryce. Because this was before the time of cellular telephones, we received several of these types of requests each week. There was nothing unusual about it.

The call was assigned to a patrol officer, and I responded to assist. It was not the type of call that generally required an assist unit but it was a rather slow day so I went along to break up the boredom. Both of us were just a couple blocks away from the house and arrived at about the same time. We found the small station wagon parked under the carport. The rear hatch was opened and a blanket was laid out neatly in the cargo compartment of the stationwagon. As we approached the car we found it was running. The situation peaked our interest but not to the point we felt there was any concern for the safety of the Duncan family.

I walked to the front door and knocked while my partner, Geoff, went to the back door. After not receiving an answer, I tried the knob and found it locked. Geoff shouted for me to come to the back yard and by the tone of his voice I knew something was not right. My pulse began to race.

I darted to the rear of the house. Geoff looked at me and then pointed to something about eight feet up in a nearby tree. I wasn't sure what it was so I walked closer. I discovered it was a pair of woman's panties and they were covered in blood.

The sunny spring day just turned grizzly.

Geoff radioed for assistance. We were not sure what we had but we both felt there was something disturbing in store. With just a nod of the head to each other, we hurried to the back door and attempted to look in the window but the view was blocked. At first I thought the window had been painted from the inside but within a few seconds I realized it was blood that obstructed our view into the kitchen. My heart began to race in fear...fear that we had a dead body and fear the suspect might still be inside.

At the risk of destroying potential evidence, I grabbed the door knob and turned it. The door was unlocked. Even the most graphic horror film could not depict what we saw when the door opened. I had been around dead bodies before due to my career, but nothing involving the blood and violence I encountered.

With service revolvers drawn, we entered the kitchen. My attention was first drawn to the amount of blood covering the linoleum floor. It seems like a silly notion now, but at the time I was afraid I was going to slip and fall. I carefully trekked across the kitchen floor to the body of a female lying on her side. I could tell she was dead and all indications were it happened within the last thirty minutes. I could see numerous deep lacerations on her face, chest and arms but what drew my attention was that at least six of her fingers were missing from what appeared to be defensive knife wounds. My nausea was only surpassed by my fear the murderer was still in the house. But I regained some courage when I thought about the five-year-old child. We directed our attention from the body to continue the search of the house for Bryce...and possibly a murderer.

As we painstakingly made our way down the hallway of the small three bedroom house, my thoughts began to wonder what kind of a son of a bitch could do such a heinous act. Was he capable of inflicting the same atrocities on a child? It was only a few seconds until I got my answer.

After searching and securing the bathroom and two bedrooms, we got to the doorway of the final bedroom. I took a quick peek into the room and in that split second saw the boy lying on the bed with his eyes opened and looking at me. I think I breathed a sigh of relief. Both Geoff and I raced into the room where we expected to grab the child from the bed and quickly remove him from the house. But that was not to be.

Just as I had observed on my quick peek, five year

old Bryce Duncan did have his eyes open and looking toward the door. But what I did not see the first time was his abdomen had been sliced open and he had been disemboweled. An involuntary gasp of surprise and revulsion escaped through my lips. It was by far the most horrendous thing I had seen in my life. The poor child had to have been awake when the torture was taking place.

I went through a roller-coaster of emotions: horror, confusion, anger, loathing. What could this child have done to deserve this? Nothing, my thoughts screamed back! That child did nothing to deserve this! I could feel the hatred emanating from my body. I looked at Geoff. We were going to catch this crazy bastard and he was going to be put away. I had heard of 'solemn vows' before. This was the first time I truly evoked one.

Geoff and I exited the house, and were met by the Chief of Detectives Chuck Sherman. We told him what we had, and he said he would take command of the investigation as was protocol. Geoff and I began to cordon off the area with crime scene tape.

Even while we tried to get our emotions under control, for Geoff and I the hard part was over. The Major Case Squad was activated and highly skilled detectives from area departments began to arrive on scene. I was detailed to direct the media to a staging area and insure they did not contaminate the crime scene.

As part of the initial investigation, Lieutenant Sherman searched the Duncan's address in our records management system for previous contacts. Most of them occurred in the last eight months and involved complaints by Linda Duncan over late night loud music coming from the Boswell house next door. It was the house on the driveway side of the Duncan residence and only twenty feet away from her running car.

While awaiting the arrival of the Crime Scene Unit, Lieutenant Sherman walked around the exterior of the Duncan residence looking for any additional evidence that would lead to a suspect. As he walked past the open bedroom window at the Boswell house he heard a somewhat familiar voice say, "Chuck, I didn't do this."

Lieutenant Sherman looked up to find a young

male standing by the bedroom window. He recognized him as twenty-year-old Johnnie Boswell. Johnnie was wearing cutoff jeans, no shirt and no shoes. He was a local dope smoker who had a remarkable resemblance to Charles Manson. Along with the loud music complaints from Linda, our previous contacts with him involved a few misdemeanor arrests for marijuana. Johnnie was what we call a "frequent flier" and we all knew him.

Now this was my first murder investigation but I will attest that none of the murders I would be involved in over the next five decades would result in the discovery of a perpetrator in less than fifteen minutes. Though police officers spend six or more months in their initial training, thousands of hours of additional training, and accumulated experience to help us to recognize and discover clues needed to solve crimes, this particular crime nearly solved itself.

The clues discovered by Lieutenant Sherman as he stood at the window talking to Johnnie would likely have been obvious to any lay person. Johnnie had a substantial amount of blood on his right abdomen that did not coincide with a wound or injury.

"What didn't you do?" Lieutenant Sherman asked.

Johnnie nodded over to the Duncan resident. "Whatever happened in there," he replied.

Lieutenant Sherman took Johnnie by the arm and had him step out of the ground level window and into the yard. When Lieutenant Sherman looked down, he observed that Johnnie's bare feet were covered in a large amount of still fresh blood. He was our suspect. Lieutenant Sherman handcuffed him and turned him over to another detective to remove him from the area and transport him to the jail.

Geoff and I were moved to a role as support staff which, fortunately, gave me time to reflect on what I had just seen. This was my first peek behind the curtain into the world of evil and darkness. I could no longer count myself among the "protected" who do not have a need or requirement to see what lies beyond the curtain. I knew it was this moment and this day that would determine if I were to continue as a police officer or seek another occupation.

I stood at the crime scene perimeter watching the coroner enter the house, the buzzing of the crime scene workers and detectives, and nervous onlookers gathered in the street. I realized it was not the indelible memory of the butchered bodies of Linda and Bryce Duncan nor the extreme sadness and anger invoked by what I saw that anchored my decision to continue in law enforcement. I saw the utter determination in the veteran cops to locate, arrest and convict the person responsible for taking these lives. I wanted to be like them. I wanted to "speak for the dead" and fight for their survivors. I wanted - no, I needed - to be a police officer. It was to become not just a job or occupation but rather a lifestyle. Many times after that day I would pull back the tainted veil and enter the world of pure evil with my fellow officers. Each time we made our way out of that world, a bit of our innocence remained behind. This is the sacrifice we make to the people we protect that they can never understand.

At the station, later in the day, Lieutenant Sherman attempted to interview Johnnie but he had nothing to say except "old lady Duncan" was always calling the police on him because he played his music too loud. He would not admit to being in the Duncan house that day or to killing

Linda and Bryce although he gave no reason for the blood on his body or the small cuts on his hands. If we were to make a case against Johnnie, we would have to do it without his assistance and that was just how it was done.

Samples of blood taken from Johnnie turned out to be Linda and Bryce Duncan blood types. Since DNA was yet to be introduced, blood types were accepted as direct evidence in most cases. Still, there was not enough evidence for a conviction.

With the issuance of a search warrant, the investigators were able to locate blood covered property taken from the Duncan house in Johnnie's bedroom. The most critical item found was an eight inch butcher knife with a broken tip and broken wooden handle that was blood covered. During an autopsy, the tip of that blade was discovered in Linda Duncan's abdomen. This was the key piece of evidence that got Johnnie convicted about thirteen months later. Unfortunately, one juror at Johnnie Boswell's trial would not accept the death penalty and Johnnie received two natural life sentences without parole. To this day, Johnnie's world remains a six foot by nine foot steel and concrete enclosure.

and ka-plooie

In my first ten years on the job, I responded to four house explosions. This was before the methamphetamine cookers blew themselves up on a regular basis. Having four houses explode in a small residential town within that span of time was like going to a large fight and finding four sober people. It just defied all odds.

One early spring day in the mid-afternoon, I was on patrol in the business district of my town when suddenly my car shook violently. I saw the plate glass windows of the stores near me disintegrate, showering the area in shards of glass.

I did not know where the explosion came from but I knew the phones would soon be ringing off the hook.

Within fifteen seconds, the dispatcher sent me to a residential area less than a mile away. The report was a house had exploded and several other neighboring houses were seriously damaged.

I was the first to arrive. The normally quiet street was covered with roof shingles and boards. Pieces of trees blocked my entrance and a heavy fog from the settling debris filled the neighborhood.

Several residents ran up to me relaying that none of them were injured but the middle aged man who lived in the house that exploded was missing.

It took me a few seconds but I recognized the house that exploded as being one that officers had been to in the past. The middle aged guy was Jake Lee. He and his wife were separated and in the process of a divorce. Since the separation began, Lee had been on a continual drunk. It was just after one in the afternoon so I'm sure he was well on his way to being falling down drunk before the explosion.

As I made my way to the house, I reported the details to the dispatcher so he could relay it to the fire department. As I stepped gingerly on the rubble to prevent injury to me or anyone trapped below, I heard a voice yell, "Officer McNally, I'm here!"

I looked around but did not see anyone. Immediately I heard the same voice say, "Officer McNally, I'm up here!"

I peered at the tree about five yards from me and then gazed up about 25 feet along the trunk. There he was, Jake Lee, with his pants around his ankles and seated on a somewhat intact toilet perched at the intersection of two tree limbs. I blinked. And blinked again. Yep...there was a grown man, on a toilet, in a tree.

Lee was extremely intoxicated which was no big surprise. Like all drunks, he continually repeated the same question over and over, "McNally, what happened?"

Each time, I told him his house exploded and that he needed to stay still until the fire department arrived to rescue him.

The fire department was on scene about three minutes after I arrived. I directed them to Lee and they began a rescue operation.

Now I will tell you the fire department continually trains on rescue techniques using a number of scenarios. As I watched, I had to wonder how many times they trained to get a drunk off a toilet located 25 feet up in a tree. Based upon what I was seeing, I'm sure someone at sometime had suggested they practice such a rescue because they were flawless in the steps that rescued Lee.

I also wondered how they kept from laughing.

Once Lee was on the ground and his pants pulled back up, the paramedics examined him. I told them I was sure he was feeling no pain but they took a look anyway. They found the victim and his "sudden rise to fame" (every camera in the neighborhood was snapping away) was without injury.

I was able to move Lee away from the crowd and ask him about the explosion. He started to sober a bit and said he now remembered what happened. He had decided to kill himself over the impending divorce. He drank a fifth and a half of Jack Daniels Whiskey then turned on the unlit burners of the gas stove. He sat in the kitchen waiting to die.

Lee said he waited two hours and nothing happened. He told me he had to "take a shit real bad" so he went to the bathroom.

What Lee described next was not likely to rival the experiences of the original Mercury astronauts but it had a great deal of entertainment value. As he sat on the toilet, he decided to have a smoke. He placed a cigarette in his mouth, flicked the lighter, and began to inhale.

The words Lee used to describe the actual event would never be as historic as those chosen by astronaut Neil Armstrong but in this small blue-collar community they would be repeated over and over at seniors' meetings, taverns, coffee clubs and high school locker rooms for several generations.

"I just went to take a shit, lit a cigarette and 'ka-ploooie' I was riding that toilet through the attic and roof. If it wasn't for the tree I would be half way into outer space by now," declared Lee.

I envisioned this drunk man with his pants around his ankles, a cigarette hanging out of the side of his mouth, and riding on a toilet as he passed through the outer reaches of Earth's atmosphere. I asked Lee if he would be willing to retell this story to a couple of my friends from NASA. He said, "Hell, yes!"

Of course I never brought someone from NASA to talk to Lee but the dispatcher did get numerous phone calls from him asking to speak with me about when they were arriving. The good thing was he didn't try to kill himself again because he was concerned NASA would show up for his story, and he wouldn't be there to speak with them.

Two Little Girls

On a mild April evening in 1978, I was patrolling a relatively quiet district in my city. There had been little activity on the radio and I was enjoying the break before the craziness that comes with summer. The one unwritten rule of police work is we never say the "Q" word or it will come back to haunt you. I had just pulled away from meeting with another officer who said how **QUIET** it was tonight. Apparently he didn't get the memo about using that word because the dispatcher came on the radio and asked me to copy an assignment. I could tell from his voice the call was something urgent. I was told to assist the fire department who was responding to a residential neighborhood on a report of a single family residence on fire with a report of persons trapped inside.

I pulled onto the highway and activated my emergency lights and siren to drive the mile to the fire. As I looked to the horizon I could see a large amount of smoke that rose into the sky in the area of the fire. Both my response speed and my heartrate increased as I wondered what I was to find upon my arrival. In less than a minute I found my answer.

The house was a single family ranch style house. I was familiar with the layout of these type houses in our town. There was fire coming from the two bedroom windows facing the street and very dense dark smoke puffing from around the frame of the front door. I put my car in park before it came to a full stop, opened the driver's door and began a full run toward the front door of the house. I noticed as I left my patrol car that another police unit was just pulling up behind my car. A screaming lady ran up to me and said there were two little girls trapped in the house. I said, "Where?" and she pointed to the bedroom window on the left end of the house where black smoke and orange flames had filled the now missing glass. The fire department was not yet on the scene.

Besides being a police officer I also helped as a volunteer fireman and had extensive training in firefighting. As I ran at full speed toward the front door, I knew that once I got in the house I would have to crawl along at floor level to have an area absent of smoke but enough air to breathe. That was the only chance I had of getting to the girls.

I stopped about three feet short of the front door and kicked it near the door knob to get it to open. At that time, I also realized another police officer was standing next to me waiting to go in the house. On the second kick, the door opened and a thick wall of black toxic smoke filled the doorway. I got down on my stomach and began to crawl in the house with the other officer following. There was about six inches of "clear" air along the floor but I knew from the heat I was feeling on my back that this clear spot was not going to last but about another minute. Then there would be no air to breathe.

I knew the basic layout of this ranch style home so I worked quickly to get to the hallway and down to the bedroom at the front of the house. It was dark from the thick black smoke but the fire had grown to an intensity that I could now see the orange flames along the ceiling. Time was not on our side. We had only seconds to find the girls and get out of the house.

I would not be embarrassed to admit I was afraid at this point but I was not. I don't consider myself a brave man by any measure. I probably have as many fears and concerns as most people I know. But at this point, I was on a "mission" to get these little girls out alive and fear was not an emotion that helped accomplish that mission. I was relying on training and experience to get us all out.

I began to feel along the bedroom floor until I grabbed what I believed to be the leg of a bed. I slid my hand up the leg to the mattress until I felt a leg. As quickly as I touched the leg, I went to my knees and ran both my arms under her torso and quickly pulled her to the small air space along the floor. Just as I got her to the floor I heard my partner say he found another little girl. We had to get out of there in a hurry but I knew there was one thing I must do first to increase this girl's chance of survival. I placed my mouth over her nose and mouth, and gave her a breath of air. As a certified EMT, I knew that would increase her chances of survival and it was worth the 3 seconds I spent of our precious time. Without a word, my partner and I began to crawl quickly toward the front door. We cradled the girls in our arms stretched out in front of us. The smoke and flames were disorienting. It would be very easy to get lost and not find our way back out. I knew this going in so I made a mental note every time we took a turn in the house on our way to the bedroom and it led us back out without any delays.

As we reached the front door, I stood up with the girl in my arms. It was the first chance I had to look at her. Part of her clothes were melted to her body. There was black soot on her face and especially her small nostrils. I knew she had inhaled some pretty dangerous smoke. I knelt down in the front yard and placed her on the ground. One of the firemen who were now on scene started to pick her up and I angrily stopped him. She was my responsibility. We had just escaped certain death. She was out of the danger of the fire and now my mission had changed. I started to assess her medically. She was not breathing and I could find no pulse. I thought to myself, "God, please don't do this". I started CPR on this child who looked to be no more than three years old. I glanced to my partner who was next to me with his little girl. He was giving her CPR also. She looked to be about five years old and physically in worse shape than my little one.

There was an ambulance on scene so I yelled to

my partner to head for the ambulance. If these girls were to survive they needed the critical care that only a trauma center could offer. We carried our girls to the ambulance, the door shut and we were on our way for the eight minute ride to the hospital. We continued the CPR and were met at the emergency entrance of the hospital by a hoard of medical personnel. They grabbed the girls, put them on stretchers and raced into the hospital. I tried to follow them but I couldn't keep up. I guess the inhalation of smoke and the exhaustion of performing CPR slowed me down.

When I got inside I went into the examination room where my little girl was. The doctors, nurses and technicians where barking orders loudly and everyone was scurrying about the room. It was a scene of controlled chaos but they had a plan. Unfortunately, they had done this before. It was only a few minutes until I heard one of them say, "She's breathing on her own". I felt a ton of stress just flow from my body. She was safe. I stepped from the room to check on my partner and the other little girl. It took only one look at him to know she didn't make it. He was devastated. We both had black soot on our faces but he had two trails from below his eyes and across his cheeks where his tears had washed away the soot.   I sat next to him in silence. There was nothing to say.

Within about a minute our attention was drawn away from our grief by the activity on our police radios. Several of our police cars were pursuing a vehicle from the area of the fire. I heard one of the officers say it was the father of the little girls and he was armed with a pistol. I was a bit confused about what was happening but was going to find out soon because another officer arrived at the hospital to give us a ride back to our police cars which were parked at the fire scene.

This officer told us a witness at the scene said she saw the girl's father walk in the front door of the house with a can of gasoline and come out a few minutes later without the can. She said he lit a lighter and threw it in the house and the flames "exploded" from the house. She said he left just before the first police car arrived. The officer stated that the father returned to the house while the firemen were trying to put out the fire and he stood in front of the house with a pistol in his hand and held the firemen at bay. He told them he wanted the house to burn. He then fired a gunshot in the ground in front of him and ran back to his car. As he left the scene a couple police cars attempted to stop him as he fled in the car with them chasing him.

We now listened to the radio and heard the father crashed the car and the officers had him in custody. In a few minutes, I arrived back at the fire scene, retrieved my patrol car and drove to the police station to get a look at the girl's father.

I arrived at the station about a minute before the officer transporting the father arrived. When he was taken from the car he was angry and yelling at the officers. He had blood running from his forehead. The blood was from either an injury due to the accident or he ran his ignorant mouth and it was a souvenir from a police officer. It really didn't matter to me which was the case.

As he was brought into the booking area he was yelling about what a "bitch" his wife was and that he wanted those two girls to die so they wouldn't grow up to be like their mother. I ran toward him with an uncontrollable rage and a lack of concern about the consequences of my actions. Two of the officers saw me coming and restrained me. It was not that they had any concern for the father but they knew if I attacked him it would likely end my career. I was whisked away by the officers and ordered by the shift commander to leave the station until given permission to return. It was some months later but I apologized to those officers for acting like that and thanked them for the action they took to save my job.

The father was eventually convicted of Aggravated Murder, Aggravated Arson and attempted Murder and was sentenced to fifty years in prison. I testified in the trial and recounted the fates of the two sisters. In the fall of that year my partner and I were awarded the Red Cross Lifesaver Award. The three paragraph framed letter detail how heroic we were in entering the house and removing the girls. I was embarrassed to be called "heroic". There were no heroes there that night. It was just two police officers doing what almost any two other police officers would have done given the circumstances. I have seen heroes. I have worked with many of them. I have attended their funerals, but I didn't see any that night. I never displayed the letter. It was put in closet and eventually made its way to a large box on a shelf in my garage.

Fun with the Hendersons

For the most part, domestic fight calls are among the most precarious for officers. When we arrive at a house, the anger that escalated between the combatants is generally redirected toward the police. There are, however, times when the domestic call is more entertaining than dangerous.

Take the case of a middle-aged husband and wife who spent nearly every night in their house getting drunk and arguing. I don't remember a time when either of them called the police directly; it was generally a neighbor or someone passing by. Every cop on the force had been to their residence multiple times. In fact, the dispatcher no longer gave out their address on calls but just said, "Disturbance at the Hendersons."

Neither Kent nor Helen Henderson were ever aggressive to the police and for that matter even towards each other. We looked forward to our five times a week visits with them but nothing topped the fun of having a rookie officer deal with the dueling couple for the first time. We would all pretend we hadn't been to this house before and would tell the rookie that he/she would be the reporting officer in the call. That meant they not only gathered the information and wrote the report, but would make decisions on the outcome of the call.

Kent always referred to Helen as "that crazy bitch who ruined my life" and she would reply with "I knew I should have married your brother." Kent would look at a rookie and say, "You're new" and then tell him not to "look at her directly in the face or you will be blinded." The other officers and I would stand to the side and do our best not to laugh.

On one particular night, the Hendersons had agreed they were going to divorce "for good." Remarkably they had decided, using what was left of the alcohol soaked left hemisphere of their brains, how to divide the property they had procured in the twenty five years of marriage.

Everything, that is, except for one item.

What was that item? A wedding ring? Antique heirloom? Pet? The item was - are you ready? - a box of Fruity Tooty cereal. Even I didn't see that one coming. The arguing became increasingly out-of-control.

The rookie had no idea where to go from there. Kent and Helen could not be managed.

It took me about three seconds until my vast police experience kicked in and gave me an obvious solution. I opened the cabinet, removed the box from the shelf, placed it gently on the kitchen floor and then jumped on it with both feet. There was a popping noise as the liner bag exploded followed immediately by the breaking of the box, and an infinite amount of small fruit colored grains flying through the kitchen.

I looked up and everyone in the room, including the Hendersons, were staring at me in disbelief.

I broke the silence by telling the Hendersons to put their hands on my badge. They knew what this meant because we performed this ritual several times a week. To the Hendersons, it meant a divorce was eminent. Not legally, of course, but that didn't seem to bother them.

Kent and Helen put their hands on my badge, and I asked them if they wanted to divorce. When they responded with "I do" then I pronounced them no longer man and wife. Those simple two words would always end the fight and the police could leave. Once the divorce was performed, we never had to return again that same night.

After the alcohol wore off, we were often called back the next evening to conduct a "marriage." It was executed in basically the same way with the hands on my badge, the "I do" being repeated, but this time the groom kissed the bride. Once again, it was not legal, and once again the Hendersons didn't seem to care.

On some occasions, officers would request that the Hendersons have a small wedding cake at the ceremony so they could have a piece before they left.

I cannot count the numbers of divorces I presided over but I will tell you it was one of the most effect ways to solve a domestic dispute...especially for the Hendersons.

Dying Declaration

When I came into this profession in the late 1970's I heard many stories from the veteran cops about the "old days". Throughout this book I will relay some of the olden days stories as told to me. This is one of them.

In the 1960's cops weren't paid very well. Please don't misunderstand, it is still not the quickest way to repay your student loans based upon other available opportunities. But back then it wasn't enough money to support a family. Most cops worked another full time job and took advantage of every economic opportunity that came their way. One of these opportunities came from R&L, a local towing company. The owner of R&L offered $5.00 to each officer for every time he towed a car for the police. Frank's Towing, the other towing service, did not offer that deal to the officers. Naturally, R&L did most of the towing.

Everyone involved accepted the arrangement and, for the most part, the operation went smoothly until one particular accident. On a late fall evening a serious accident happened at

Spring Street and Route 63. The officers arrived and found both cars involved in the accident were nearly unrecognizable. Officer Stepniak was the reporting officer so he began to sort through the details of what happened. He recognized one of the drivers who was deceased. Stepniak knew this was the brother-in-law of Frank from Frank's Towing. Nonetheless he had the dispatcher contact R&L Towing to remove both cars from the scene. After all, "that's five bucks" he would later recount. R&L Towing came to the accident, removed both cars and Officer Stepniak finished both his report and his shift. All was well until the next day.

When Stepniak was arriving the next afternoon to begin his shift, he saw Frank and family leaving the police station. As he entered the police station, Stepniak was met by a red faced, angry Chief Flemming who got within an inch of his face and said, "You son-of-a-bitch. What the hell were you thinking by calling R&L? Don't tell me you didn't recognize Frank's son-in-law."

Now Officer Stepniak was a cool and calm kind of guy. He never had highs or lows but just maintained a steady straight forward demeanor. Even when facing down his boss, there was no change in his expression as he looked the Chief directly in the face and said, "When I got there he was still alive. He looked up at me and said, 'Have R&L tow my car' and then he died." The veins strained to break through the Chief's forehead as he yelled, "BULLSHIT". With the calmness of a man sleeping in church Officer Stepniak said, "Prove it" and walked away.

Your Tax Dollars at Work

When Congress passes funding bills, it is sometimes hard to discover exactly where the money is going and for what purpose. One hot August night I was able to get some insight as to where my tax money was going.

It was about 1:30 in the morning, and I received a call that a female was just pushed out of a moving car onto the highway, and the car continued speeding southbound. Our dispatcher contacted the town just south of us with a vehicle description as I proceeded to the scene where the female was located.

About the time I arrived, I got a radio call from the other town saying they had the car stopped and would be transporting them back to the scene.

In the meantime I got out and spoke with the well-dressed female. She had some abrasions on her hands, knees and shoulders but nothing that was severe in nature.

As I began to speak with her, something caught my attention. It was her Adam's apple. It was protruding more than most women, and as she spoke there was a somewhat deep tone in her voice. Thinking I was just imagining this, I continued to get her story.

She said a couple of guys picked her up in a bar in my town. She got in the car with one of them driving and the other in the back seat with her. The guy with her was kissing her, and eventually had exposed her breasts and was groping them. She said he suddenly got angry, began cursing at her, then opened the back door pushing her out onto the highway while the car was still moving. She said she had no idea why he became so angry. Sensing there was more to this story, I awaited the arrival of the other officer and the suspects.

When they arrived, I first spoke with the driver. He said they picked up this girl in a bar and was taking her to a motel. Then his friend suddenly opened the rear door and pushed her from the car. He said he had no idea why his he did this. The friend was the key to what happened as neither the female or the driver provided much information.

I moved the friend away from everyone else and prefaced my question with, "Be honest with me or I'll lock you up." I then asked him what happened.

Apparently he and his friend picked up the girl, and she agreed to go to a motel with them. While his friend was driving, he was in the back seat kissing the girl and fondling her breasts. He said he reached to her crotch area and discovered - to his surprise - that "she" had a penis. To quote him, "She had a penis...a larger penis than me so I opened the car door and kicked her out."

I immediately thought if the criteria for kicking people out of a moving car is they have a larger penis then me, it looks like I'm not going to be driving in the High Occupancy Vehicle lane much.

But anyway...

I went back to the shim (she/him) and asked what she wanted done in this matter. She said she needed $50 to replace her torn clothing and if the men were willing to give her the money, she would sign a refusal to prosecute form. It was agreed and the men gave her $50.

Prior to her leaving, she exposed her breasts and said the government paid for the implants. I was a bit curious about what department of the government sponsored the free boobies. I was quite sure it wasn't Department of Defense because they provided no protection as evidenced by the abrasions on her body. It couldn't have been Department of Transportation because she wasn't able to sustain a ride with them.

So I finally considered the Executive Branch of our fine government. Maybe somebody from the West Wing. They would be the only officials who wouldn't notice two out of place boobs.

I was truly dumbfounded when she displayed my tax dollars at work. All I could say to her was, "And I was just hoping to get a few potholes filled."

Until Death Do Us Part

I've said before and still contend that one of the most difficult functions of a police officer is to deliver death notifications to family members. It is at the moment you notify the family of the death of a loved one I can almost see the end of life as they knew it before this moment and the beginning of a new reality without decedent. Some people never get past that moment. The notification that a terminally ill or elderly relative had passed is not as traumatic as an unexpected passing. The unexpected the deaths were exponentially more difficult to deliver as were they to receive by the family. The most difficult notification I made was a perfect storm of all the things I would not wish on my worst enemy.

We were dispatched and arrived on the scene of a multiple fatality accident. There were numerous first responders on scene dealing with the crash. As I walked toward one of the mangled vehicles, I stopped to pick up a bible lying in the roadway. Several pages were marked for quick access, much like I see my pastor at church doing in preparation for gospel readings. A folded flyer stuck out of the bible. I tucked the Bible under my arm and continued my walk to the car. As I arrived, one of the officers told me there was a middle aged man in a tuxedo and a young girl in a wedding dress in that car. They both died in the crash.

As quickly as possible, we obtained identification on the two. It appeared it was a father and his daughter. I remembered the flyer in the Bible and opened it. The girl was a bride-to-be. The flyer said the wedding was to start in about 30 minutes from now. But it wouldn't. The bride and the proud father who was to give her away were dead.

Our department chaplain Father Jim was riding with one of the officers in another patrol district. I called on the radio and had him meet me at the accident. When he arrived I told him, "Padre, we have one helluva mess here". I always restrained my normal "police language" around the father in respect to his position. I told him that he and I need to go to this church and notify then family about then deaths. I could tell he didn't like this any more than I but time was not on our side.

We left the accident for the twenty minute ride to the church. I don't remember either of us saying a word on the trip. I know I was struggling in my mind with the words I would use to relay this horrible news and I'm sure Father Jim was having similar thoughts. Before I realized it we were pulling onto the parking lot. A few people glanced at us with a mild curiosity but did not seem to be alarmed. I, on the other hand, knew what I had to say in a few minutes would permanently change some of their lives.

Father Jim and I parked close to the front of the church. It was about five minutes before the scheduled ceremony was to begin. I hoped we could enter the vestibule and make contact with the pastor and notify him first. We opened the front door of the church and found it entered directly into the worship area. We were surrounded by finely dressed young ladies and men who were part of the wedding party. If it could not get worse, the entire congregation was looking toward the entrance in anticipation of the ceremony beginning. I could have been standing there naked and would not feel any more out of place.

The faces of curiosity I had seen moments ago were now seated in the church but the curiosity was quickly overtaking the crowd and being replaced with a concern for the presence of Father and me. Without being a clairvoyant, I was able to know the immediate future as it related to those gathered. I did not control their future but I held the knowledge of what was next to come.

I asked for the groom and he came toward me. I asked him if the mother of the bride was present and he immediately summoned her. I saw the pastor walking toward us and I motioned for all of us to step away from everyone else. Though Father Jim was there to help, unfortunately it was my job to inform the families of the deaths. Clearly the expression on my face led them to believe there was some sad news. I'm quite sure they never expected what I had to say.

I looked directly at the groom and the bride's mother and said, "There has been a car accident". The mother immediately said, "How bad are they hurt?" She knew my message was about her husband and daughter. God love her for her optimism but I couldn't make this any harder by mixing words. I said, "They did not survive." It was the best and most direct words I could use. The groom lost all color in his face and just stood without movement or sound. The mother screamed so loudly it could be heard in the parking lot.

The entire church now knew something tragic had happened. I'm sure from the mother's reaction they knew it involved death. I didn't know if she had any other children but I could almost see the last ounce of joy leave her heart when she found out her husband and daughter were gone. I wanted to grab her and hug her but that is not what we do. It would have been as much for me as her. I took a step back and the pastor grabbed the mother by the shoulders as her knees weakened and were no longer able to hold her. Father Jim turned to the groom as the reality of my words began to show in his reactions.

I took another step back as an older man approached me. He said he was the father of the groom. He overheard what I just told his son. I quickly handed him my card with my cell phone number. My experience in these cases is that after I leave, the family has many questions concerning the event and what to do going forward. I told the father that he and other family members could call me "anytime" and I would answer the questions I could or find someone who could give them those answers. In these cases an officer cannot just go off duty for a few days and leave the family to fend for themselves.

I then turned and left the church. I knew Father Jim would be out when enough friends took control of helping the family. I sat in the car a moment and said a prayer for the family of the bride and her father. It was they who needed the help now and the days to come would be most difficult. I would never forget their faces when I told them the terrible news and they would remain constantly on my mind for a few weeks until I had to do it all over again when I told grandparents that the boyfriend of their drug addicted daughter beat their three year old grandson to death with his fists.

You feel sympathy and empathy for the survivors but you cannot take on their pain and loss. I cannot turn back time and make it not happen. I cannot fix their lives. I can only interact with them in a manner that does not add to their pain. Then I must go and prepare to do it all over again. This is how we keep our sanity. Officers who don't subscribe to this routine generally quit the job within a few years.

Amazing Grace

I have sometimes found it necessary when encountering a particularly disturbing call to void myself of all emotional connection and view the situation as though I were an observer rather than a participant. There are, however, events that are so emotionally overwhelming that we are just drawn into them no matter how we resist. This is one of those few times I, against all attempts to resist, became emotionally involved.

It was a warm and humid mid-western summer night. Dispatch was already prioritizing calls because it was clear we did not have enough officers to handle the minor incidents. I was dispatched to a roll-over accident in a rural area of the county. I knew that the general location of the accident was not an area of much vehicle traffic and even fewer residences. The sheriff's department dispatcher continued to relay updated information to me as I responded with emergency lights and siren. He said the caller did not remain on scene but observed an SUV about 30 yards off the roadway with extensive damage and smoke coming from the vehicle. Fire rescue was being dispatched but no other sheriff units were available to assist. No problem, I've handled thousands of accident in the past. Why would this be different, I thought? I was the first emergency unit to arrive on scene and was soon to find a shocking answer to my question.

I could see the dimmed taillights of the SUV about 100 feet from the roadway in a heavily wooded area. I advised dispatch I was on scene and asked them to have fire rescue and paramedics expedite. With flashlight in hand, I moved as quickly as I could along the path taken by the SUV. I stumbled over broken trees and limbs, along the way noticing recently deposited beer cans under my feet. I was far from surprised this accident involved both alcohol and speed, and I prepared myself to see one or more dead people when I got to my destination.

About the time I arrived at the SUV, I was breathing heavily from the safari like trek. Just a quick look inside the vehicle and I was sure the three males and one female did not survive the impact. It didn't appear any of the four were out of their teens yet but this was no time to get emotional. I had a JOB to do. I needed to have a coroner come to the scene to pronounce these kids as dead. But before I did that, I needed to take a closer look at each them to make sure they were, in fact, beyond medical help.

As the driver's side of the SUV was closest to me, I checked him first. As I stood next to the SUV, I could smell that familiar odor of blood and alcohol mix that I have come to know so well. It had become to me a nauseating odor that signaled serious injury and death. Unfortunately, I knew this wouldn't be the last time that smell would enter my nose. My examination continued and I discovered the driver had a severe cut across his neck. From the amount of blood on and around him, he likely bled to death.

The back seat driver's side passenger had his left arm severed with the part just below his elbow hanging on by a small piece of skin tissue. My experience with this type of injury is that blood would be squirting from the opened artery if his heart was still beating. It wasn't. Clearly he was dead too.

I struggled to get between some downed tree

limbs to get to the passenger side of the car but with some difficulty I arrived at the passenger side rear of the car to find another young man dead. There was a separation in his skin and skull across his forehead and a significant amount of brain matter was exposed with some visible on the headrest in front of him.

Before reaching the front passenger seat, my thoughts began to wonder and with a mostly selfish thought I began to think about how I was going to tell the parents that their children will not be coming home....forever. It is one of the truly worst things we have to do. There is no good way to give such devastating news to a parent. I was told in the academy that death notifications were a part of our job but no one told us how to do it. I had yet in 25 plus years to find an easy or reliable way to deliver this information.

I was able to determine the best way to tell a parent is to not be the one telling them. Most of us figured out if we located a family's chaplain, used the department assigned chaplain or located a close friend or neighbor, they could deliver the sad news. Although, no matter who delivered the news, you were there to see the terror and disbelief on their faces as that moment in their lives is frozen in time and you become a part of the still picture that will be viewed so often in their nightmares. I will have to deal with that later. Back to the task at hand. I had one more person to check.

As I worked my way to the front seat, I saw a teenaged girl. She was bent forward at the waist with her face embedded in the windshield. From her mid-thigh to her feet, the SUV had collapsed around her from the impact with a tree. I pulled back the collar of her blood soaked blouse to check for a pulse. As I touched her neck, her right arm moved slightly. It was the only part of her body that was not mangled or pinned from the wreck.

I wasn't sure if she was conscious but I began to speak to her in case she could hear me. I said, "Stay with me, dear. We are going get you out of here". The words were coming out of my mouth but I knew it was not likely she was going to be freed before she lost the battle to her injuries. "We" I said. There was no "we". It was just me with no medical supplies or extrication tools. I was going to stand here helplessly and watch this girl die. I said to myself, "I hate this damned job".

No more had I told the girl I was there to help when she weakly said, "Daddy, I'm so sorry. I love you". Oh my God! This poor dying girl thinks I am her father but what am I to do? Do I tell her I'm a police officer or do I continue as her father? I had just seconds to decide. Is it morally wrong to pretend to be this girl's father? I thought of my daughter who was not much younger than this girl. It became clearly evident to me at that moment that I could do more for this young lady as a father than a police officer.

I took her blood covered hand and said," That's okay, honey. I love you too". She mumbled something but I could not hear her. I responded by telling her how much her mother and I love her, and how blessed we are to be her parents. As I continued to talk, I felt her grip relax. The last remnants of life just left her body. She was dead. With only a few short words in the last three minutes of her life, this young lady reminded me the most important things in life....be sorry for what you do to others....and love someone.

"Peace be with you," I said as I gently released her hand. My police officer responsibilities had completely escaped me as I stood there as a father who had just lost his daughter. The tears ran down my cheek as I sat on the ground, too weak to stand. I don't know how long I sat there but at some point I heard the sound of sirens in the distance. I stood and wiped the tears from my cheeks with my blood soaked hands and slowly walked back toward the road. A realization hit me. It was clear this was going to be my last shift as a police officer. I had seen too many ugly things and this was to be my last.

I spent the next several hours at the accident scene as fire rescue extricated the bodies from the vehicle, placed them in the road and covered them with brightly colored tarps. I located identification on each of the bodies. Her name was Grace. How appropriate I thought because she left this world with such grace. Before she was taken from the scene I found a moment to kneel next to her and whisper, "Thank you, Grace". I had no idea why I chose those words but it just seemed to be the right thing to say.

Because of the workload I had detailing this

accident, the coroner said he would make notifications to the family. I was so relieved because I did not want to see Grace's family. I couldn't tell them I found her alive and what she said but I also could not lie to them. No one, including the coroner, asked if any of the four were alive when I arrived so I did not volunteer that information.

I called off sick for my shift the next night. I had nothing left to give. Tens of thousands of cops would be out there tonight protecting a public who has no idea what we do and see every night. I just couldn't be one of them. It was my intent to resign my commission the next day. I could not see another ugly thing.

Later the next evening, I dozed off a few minutes after being up for nearly two days. I had no recollection of any dream or nightmare but when I awoke I had a peaceful content feeling. I now understood why I said, "Thank you, Grace". I realized it was Grace that made me see the importance of what we do as police officers. For just three short minutes our lives intersected and I thought it was I who arrived to help Grace but in fact Grace was there to teach me the value of the impact we have on other's lives. The last thing she gave was a lesson in humanity to an old and tired cop.

 I've had nearly twenty years of police service since Grace's death but the time with her remains as vivid to me as any event in my police career. Whenever I begin to doubt the impact that I and my fellow officers have on those we have sworn to serve, I need only say "Grace" under my breath and I'm reminded of a humid summer night I was taught a lesson in humanity by a dying young girl. **Thank You, Grace!**

About the Author

In many technical books, it is important to understand the author's educational and practical experience to weigh their qualifications to address the subject. This book is based upon my work experience and subsequent recollection of events. I have no desire to add an "I Love Me" page to the book. I will, as a matter of understanding, tell you how my life progressed to arrive at this point.

I was born into a lower middle class family and eventually had five siblings. We did not have a lot of money, but I never knew it. My wardrobe consisted hand-me-down clothes from my older brother. I never owned a pair of blue jeans that did not have patches on the knees. I could see the pavement from the floorboard of our car and I thought that was neat. My grade school teachers said I talked too much (nothing has changed there). In the summer, I left my house in the morning to go play baseball with my friends and returned "before the street lights came on."

I rode my bicycle without a helmet. I ran in the fog behind the mosquito sprayer truck. I brushed off my sandwich after I dropped it in the dirt and ate it. My mom made us lemonade on hot summer days. As a child I hated my brothers and sisters to the degree I now love them.

I left home after I graduated high school and became a paratroop in the U.S. Army. I've been married over 40 years and we have two wonderful children. Being a rebel child from the 60's, I decided to become a police officer so I could do the things my parents told me not to do - stand in the street when cars are coming, say bad words, play with guns, and talk back to adults.

I have worked as a uniformed officer, detective, homicide investigator and shift supervisor. I believe the best police departments are a part of the community and not apart from the community. My goal each shift is not to do things right but to do the right thing. I treat everyone as

I want to be treated until they indicate otherwise to me.

That is all!

Questions, comments or inquiries about the book

kmcg5555@gmail.com

CPSIA information can be obtained
at www.ICGtesting.com
Printed in the USA
LVOW12s2153110416
483160LV00028B/615/P